Copyright 2020 by Danilo Olson -All

No part of this publication may be reproduced, distributed, or transmitted in any form or by any means, including photocopying, recording, or other electronic or mechanical methods, without the prior written permission of the publisher, except in the case of brief quotations embodied in reviews and certain other non-commercial uses permitted by copyright law.

This Book is provided with the sole purpose of providing relevant information on a specific topic for which every reasonable effort has been made to ensure that it is both accurate and reasonable. Nevertheless, by purchasing this Book you consent to the fact that the author, as well as the publisher, are in no way experts on the topics contained herein, regardless of any claims as such that may be made within. It is recommended that you always consult a professional prior to undertaking any of the advice or techniques discussed within. This is a legally binding declaration that is considered both valid and fair by both the Committee of Publishers Association and the American Bar Association and should be considered as legally binding within the United States.

CONTENTS

INTRODUCTION 6
Chapter 1: Cooking Notes 8
Chapter 2: Instant Pot Recipes 11
Beef 11
    Instant Pot Short Ribs 11
    Garlic Prime Rib 12
    Braised Beef Shanks 13
    Corned Beef 14
    Beef Steak (Lemon or Seasoned) 15
    Garlic Beef 16
    Simple Beef Roast 16
    Ginger Short Ribs 17
    Instant Pot Rib Roast 17
    Grilled Beef Tenderloin 18
    Caribbean Beef 19
    Herbed Sirloin Tip Roast 20
    Gingered Beef Tenderloin 20
    Simple Shredded Beef 21
    Delicious Braised Short Ribs 22
    Pot Roast 22
    Sage Beef 23
    Oregano Spiced Beef Chops 24
    Tasty Beef Brisket 25
    Instant Pot Beef Steak 26
Chicken 27
    Simple Roast Chicken 27
    Garlicky Greek Chicken 28

Classic Lemon Chicken 29

Instant Pot Garlic Chicken 30

Whole Roasted Chicken with Lemon and Rosemary 30

Easy Asian Chicken 31

Smoky Paprika Chicken 31

Slow Cooked Chicken Drumstick 32

Slow Cooked Spiced Whole Chicken 32

Instant Pot Crispy Chicken 33

Filipino Chicken 34

Roasted Chicken 35

Lemon Herb Whole Chicken 36

Barbecue Wings 37

Shredded Chicken Breast 37

Curried Chicken 38

Italian Chicken Thighs 38

Mojo Chicken 39

Italian Shredded Chicken 39

Tasty Simple Chicken Thighs 40

Pork 41

Mustard Pork Chops 41

Leyna's Blend Pork Chops 42

Basil-Lime Carnitas 43

Asian Lemongrass Pork 44

Lemon Rosemary Pork Medallions 45

Garlic Loin Chops 46

Smothered Pork Chop 47

Adobo Pork Chops 48

Smokey and Spicy Instant Pot Roast 48

Delicious Pork Chops 49

Kalua Pork 50

- Pork Carnitas 51
- Mexican Pulled Pork 52
- Italian Pork Cutlets 52
- Mexican Chili Pork 53
- Indian Instant Pot Slow Roasted Pork 53
- Slow Cook Garlic Pork Tenderloin 54
- BBQ Baby Back Ribs 55
- Braised Pork Belly 56
- Smoked Pork Shoulder 57

Turkey 58
- Saucy Turkey Drumsticks 58
- Herbed Mayonnaise Roast Turkey 59
- Aromatic Turkey 60
- Easy Turkey Roast 61
- Garlicky and Lemony Turkey 62
- Smoked Slow-Cooked Turkey 63
- Spiced Turkey 64
- Sweet Turkey Drumsticks 65
- Buttered Turkey Breast 66
- Turkey Leg with Garlic 67
- Turkey Breast with Gorgonzola Sauce 68
- Instant Turkey Breast 69
- Turmeric Turkey Breast 70
- Basil Turkey Breast 70
- Classic Honey Turkey 71
- Rosemary Turkey 72
- Instant Pot Turkey Breast Tenderloin 73
- Instant Pot Rotisserie Turkey Legs 74
- Tasty Turkey Bites 75
- Yummy Turkey Thighs 76

Fish 77

- Poached Salmon 77
- Sockeye Salmon 78
- Dijon Halibut 79
- Smoked Codfish with Scallions 79
- Salmon Meatballs Soup 80
- Steamed Lemon Salmon 81
- Salmon with Basil Pesto 82
- Super Simple Quick Shrimp 82
- Steamed Chilli-Rubbed Tilapia 83
- Lemon Dill Salmon 84
- Foil Pack Salmon 85

Lamb 86

- Lamb Stew with Bacon 86
- Rosemary Lamb 87
- Chili Lamb Leg 88
- Crispy Garlic Lamb Chops 89
- Lamb Riblets 90
- Heavy Balsamic Lamb Shoulder 91
- Ginger Lamb 92
- Spicy Pulled Lamb 93
- Braised Lamb Shanks (Contains more than normal carbs) 94
- Classic Lamb Tagine 95

INTRODUCTION

If you're looking for straight forward easy to follow recipes to use for the carnivore diet in an instant pot than you're in luck. I wrote this book not only for you, but also for myself. I'm not a fan of sifting through ads and fluff that make up a majority of recipe's on the internet. So I wanted a go to instant pot cookbook that was not only streamlined and to the point, but also easy to follow. Believe me when I say I'll be happily placing the first order of this book in paperback just so I can have all my recipes for easy access.

I do most if not all the cooking in my house, so I know the struggle of balancing work and trying to feed my family. A great advantage of the carnivore diet is that it's easy to adjust for others in a household who aren't following the diet. Simply add a carb source (instant mash, rice), some veggies, and bam you just fed everyone else, while still sticking to your diet. And with the instant pot, you can easily cook a whole other dish while your carnivore meal is cooking. The carnivore diet with the instant post is truly the easiest diet to prepare and stick too.

This is why the instant pot is my favorite kitchen device for following the carnivore diet. Dishes like roasts or whole chickens can have their cooking time cut in half without sacrificing flavor. Not to mention the convenience of setting food start times and "keep warm" functions. These recipes included have been field tested and certainly put my instant pot to work. So if your instant pot has been lying dormant, prepare to dust it off and put it back to work.

Why the instant pot is my go to cooking device?

Grills add unique flavor and are easy to literally fire up, but they come with some trade offs. The jury is still out as to how "bad" grilling meat actually is. There has been research showing that meat cooked on the grill can be carcinogenic either from the smoke and or the charring of the meat. Personally I'm not too concerned if the meat is not burnt and if you only grill on occasion. But another major disadvantage to grilling is the cost. Using propane or charcoal to cook your food will add extra cost to cooking your food.

Cast Iron is a favorite among the carnivore community and for good reason. Simply heat a pan and throw on the meat. However it too has its disadvantages. A primary one is that it can get messy. Any veteran of cast iron cooking knows the right of passage to cleaning grease splattering and smoke stained cabinets above the stove. The latter is why wife finally banned indoor steak cooking, that is unless it's in the instant pot.

Finally it's hard to compete with a regular kitchen oven. They've stood the test of time, have plenty of space, and are relatively easy for cooking. Where the instant pot stands out above the regular oven is its speed of cooking, timer set cooking, "keep warm" function, and again easy cleanup.

Chapter 1: Cooking Notes

Special Notes about Carnivore Friendly Condiments and Toppings.
True that the carnivore diet is meat centric diet, but that doesn't mean that you can't add toppings. In fact there's no diet god that will punish you for adding something that fits your lifestyle. It's also true that most who recommend the carnivore diet will say to do so in a strict fashion eliminating everything except meat, salt, and water. The logic behind this is that by doing this you can identify any food sensitivities and do a true reset to your system.

Personally I feel that this approach makes sense if you're suffering from some of unidentified food intolerance or digestion issues, but for myself and others who have no known symptoms, a sustainable adjustment works well. I'm not saying go crazy on the sauces and spices, but a guaranteed way to ensure you won't stick with this diet is to make the diet bland and boring.

Along with this comes the concern in the carnivore community over lectins and oxalates found in some spices such as nutmeg, mustard seek, black pepper, chili powder / flakes and nutmeg to name a few. Again I'd revert back to my statement above. Desperate issues call for desperate measures. If you're struggling and think it may be food intolerance related, by all means be strict about your condiment choices. But please be careful not to assume anything not meat will harm you based on some article on the internet.

While I've attempted to keep theses recipes as simple as possible using common household spices and ingredients, some of them are questionably used among the carnivore community. These include things such as light uses of garlic and squeezed lemon to name a few. In my opinion (and the opinion of others in the carnivore community) if you're not suffering from any food intolerance issues these subtle additions will not have a negative impact and only barely add to the carb value of about 2-3 grams per serving at most. I've have tried where possible to mark substitutions and options. Most if not all of these recipes you can simply just exclude.

Just as in my previous book "The Cheap Carnivore Diet", a focus of this book is to focus on sustainability while following the carnivore diet. I want you make your carnivore journey easy and most importantly, satisfying.

Ultimately, while there is a good deal of high sugar rubs and spices, the majority are likely ok and won't cause any issues.

You may notice that there's a number of commonly used ingredients for various recipes. Below is a list of some of the spices and ingredients to have on hand. Many of these are generally accepted tolerated spices for most people following the carnivore diet.

Pepper

Red Pepper
Basil
Bay Leaf
Sage
Thyme
Dill
Cilantro
Chives
Onion (Fresh or Powder)
Paprika
Curry Powder
Coriander
Mustard
Oregano
Garlic (Fresh and Powder)
Ginger (Fresh and Powder)
Lemon & Lemon Juice
Rosemary
Beef and Chicken Stock

Iodized Salt: I have to stress this point, I don't care if its pink Himalayan sea salt or salt purified from the beaches of Fuji, if it doesn't have iodine get something else. Iodine is an essential nutrient and extremely important. Salt manufactures save a few bucks removing this so **MAKE SURE YOU HAVE IT IN YOUR SALT!** But even if you don't have access do note that many the spices add naturally contain iodine such as cinnamon, garlic, red pepper, pepper, curry powder, and parsley to name a few.

All purpose Mixed Seasoning: If you want to make a lot of these recipes even simpler, just find an a good all purpose seasoning that you enjoy.

Here are some I recommend:

[Paleo Powder All purpose seasoning](#)
[Kosmos Q Anything Seasoning](#)
[Kosmos Q Dirty Bird BBQ Rub](#)
[Celtic Sea Salt Seaweed](#) Seasoning Contains Iodine (Don't worry doesn't taste like seaweed)

Sugar free condiments: There are many companies that make sugar free alternatives to popular sauces like honey mustard, BBQ, or even sweet and sour. You'll see some recipes in this book that call for sugar free BBQ. Below are some links to sugar free seasonings I recommend.

[G Hughes Sugar Free Ketchup and BBQ Sauce](#)
[Lillie's Q Zero Sugar BBQ](#)

<u>Primal Kitchen BBQ and Steak Sauce</u>

Oil

This is another touchy topic in the carnivore community. Some recipes you can actually omit it. Unless it's a fatty cut of meat or there's liquid added, then you will need to add some sort of oil to prevent the meat from sticking to the pot.

Most in the carnivore community will say steer completely away from vegetable oil. I agree for the most part however some recipes simply taste better in flavor with a tiny bit extra virgin olive oil. Whatever you oil you choose, always make sure its of excellent quality.

Here's a list of commonly accepted carnivore oils:

Beef Tallow
Lard (includes bacon grease)
MCT Oil
Coconut Oil
Butter (can cause issues for those with food sensitivities)
Ghee

Serving Sizes & Calorie / Macro Count

I debated on keeping or leaving the servings and calories in the book, but in the end I figured it would give this book a bit for versatility. If you're following the carnivore diet then you know that your "serving size" will have to be much greater to sustain yourself. My recommendation is to just ignore the servings and eat until you're full. For the calories and macros in each recipe, I would still simply ignore them if you're following the carnivore diet. And do note that these are approximations. You may find it useful to check the carb count, but feel free to just alter or takeout the carb course in the recipe to get this down to zero. There are only a couple that actually require carbohydrates in the form of <5g.

Chapter 2: Instant Pot Recipes

Beef

Instant Pot Short Ribs

Total time: 1 hour 45 minutes
Servings: 6

Ingredients:
- 4 lbs. beef short ribs
- 2 tbsps. olive oil (or oil of choice)
- 1 sliced leek
- Salt
- 2 sliced garlic cloves
- 1 cup water
- Black pepper
- 1 sprig thyme
- 1 sprig rosemary

Directions:
1. Place all ingredients in the inner pot.
2. Secure the lid. Choose the "Manual" mode and cook for 90 minutes at High pressure. Once cooking is complete, use a natural pressure release; carefully remove the lid.
3. Afterwards, place the short ribs under the broiler until the outside is crisp or about 10 minutes.
4. Transfer the ribs to a serving platter and enjoy!

Nutritional Info:
Calories: 655, Fat: 50.8g, Carbs: 2.1g. Protein: 43.7g

Garlic Prime Rib

Total time: 50 minutes
Servings: 10

Ingredients:
- 4 lbs. prime rib roast
- 10 minced garlic cloves
- 2 tsps. dried thyme.
- 2 tbsps. oil of your choosing
- Black pepper
- Salt

Directions:
1. Select the Sauté button on the Instant Pot and heat the oil. Sauté the garlic for a minute until fragrant.
2. Add the prime rib roast and sear all sides for 3 minutes.
3. Apply pepper and salt for seasoning. Sprinkle with thyme.
4. Pour in a cup of water and remove the browning at the bottom.
5. Put on the lid and seal off the vent.
6. While on Manual option, set timer to 45 minutes.
7. Do natural pressure release.

Nutritional info:
Calories: 776, Fat: 66.5g, Carbs: 1.4 g, Protein: 40.6g

Braised Beef Shanks

Total time: 45 minutes
Servings: 4

Ingredients:
- 1½ lbs. beef shank
- 1 tsp. minced garlic
- 1 tbsp. sesame oil for flavor or carnivore oil of your choosing
- 2 tbsps. soy sauce
- 1 tsp. Chinese five spice powder (or seasonal powder of your choice)
- 1 dried red chili
- 2 cloves star anise (optional)
- 1 cup water

Directions:
1. Add all ingredients to the inner pot.
2. Secure the lid. Choose the "Manual" mode and cook for 30 minutes at High pressure. Once cooking is complete, use a natural pressure release for 10 minutes; carefully remove the lid.
3. Slice across the grain and serve over hot cooked rice if desired. Enjoy!

Nutritional Info:
Calories: 316, Fat: 11.4g, Carbs: 1.6g, Protein: 39.2g

Corned Beef

Total time: 1hour 40 minutes
Servings: 4

Ingredients:
- 3 lbs. corned beef brisket
- 12 oz. beer (Ultra light beer) or replace with chicken broth
- Pepper.
- 3 crushed minced garlic cloves (optional)
- Salt

If it's a premed mix just follow the cook time.

Directions:
1. Pour water and beer into the Instant Pot.
2. Add garlic and mix.
3. Put the steamer basket inside.
4. Season corned beef with salt and pepper.
5. Add to the basket.
6. Cover the pot.
7. Cook at high pressure for 90 minutes.
8. Release pressure quickly.
9. Transfer beef to a baking pan and cover it with foil.
10. Let it rest for 15 minutes before slicing and serving.

Nutritional info:
Calories: 417, Fat: 28.3g, Carbs: 4.9g, Protein: 27.7g

Beef Steak (Lemon or Seasoned)

Total time: 22 minutes
Servings: 2

Ingredients:
- ½ tsp. garlic salt
- 2 tbsps. lemon juice or select your choice of seasoning
- 1 tbsp. carnivore oil of your choosing
- 2 beef steaks (short loin or top loin)
- 1 crushed garlic clove

Directions:
1. Take the Instant Pot and place over dry kitchen surface; open its top lid and switch it on.
2. Press "SAUTÉ".
3. Add and heat the oil in the instant pot
4. Add the meat and salt; stir-cook for 4-5 minutes to evenly brown.
5. Add the garlic and cook for 1-2 minutes.
6. Serve with lemon juice on top.

Nutritional info:
Calories: 86, Fat: 7g, Carbs: 2g, Protein: 2g

Garlic Beef

Total time: 22 minutes
Servings: 4

Ingredients:
- Extra virgin olive oil or carnivore oil of your choosing
- 1½ lbs. beef sirloin
- 1 tbsp. sea salt
- 5 garlic cloves

Directions:
1. Rub beef with salt.
2. Peel garlic and finely-chop.
3. Add 4 tbsps. oil to Instant Pot.
4. Turn slow cooker to Sauté mode on normal and when it reads heat, add beef and sauté until browned.
5. Add garlic and sauté for 30 seconds.
6. Turn your pot to High Pressure Cook setting and set timer for 10 minutes with natural release

Nutritional info:
Calories: 402, Carbs: 1.4g, Fat: 6g, Protein: 29g

Simple Beef Roast

Total time: 1hour 10 minutes
Servings: 6

Ingredients:
- Extra virgin olive oil or carnivore oil of your choosing
- 2 cups beef stock
- 2 tbsps. salt
- 3 lbs. beef chuck roast
- 6 peppercorns

Directions:
1. Crush your peppercorns.
2. Rub meat with salt and peppercorns.
3. Coat Instant Pot and turn Sauté setting on high.
4. Once high, brown all sides of roast.
5. Turn setting to pressure cooker and add remaining ingredients, cook on normal for 60 minutes.
6. Allow for normal release.

Nutritional info:
Calories: 389, Carbs: 0.1g, Fat: 21g, Protein: 34g

Ginger Short Ribs

Total time: 35 minutes

Servings: 6

Ingredients:
- Extra virgin olive oil or carnivore oil of your choosing
- 1 large onion or 1 tbsp of onion powder
- 1 tsp. salt
- 4 beef short ribs
- 1 ginger piece or tsp of ground ginger powder

Instructions:
1. Peel your onion and dice it.
2. Peel ginger and grate it.
3. Lightly coat Instant Pot and turn setting to sauté.
4. Add in 3 tbsps of oil and heat, add onion, ginger, sauté for a minute, and add ribs and brown.
5. Change setting to pressure cooker add ¾ cup water and cook on normal for 25 minutes.
6. Allow for normal release, top with short rib, cook.
7. Serve and enjoy

Nutritional info:
Calories: 454, Carbs: 2g, Fat: 18g, Protein: 29g

Instant Pot Rib Roast

Total time: 55 minutes

Servings: 12

Ingredients:
- Pepper
- Salt
- 1 bay leaf
- 5 lbs. beef rib roast
- 1 tsp. garlic powder

Directions:
1. Place all ingredients in the Instant Pot.
2. Pour a cup of water.
3. Put on the lid and seal off the vent.
4. While on Manual option, set timer to 50 minutes.
5. Do natural pressure release.

Nutritional info:
Calories: 601, Fat: 52.2g, Carbs: 0.5g, Protein: 32.3g

Grilled Beef Tenderloin

Total time: 35 minutes
Servings: 6

Ingredients:
- 1 tbsp. butter or ghee
- 1 tbsp. olive oil or carnivore oil of your choosing
- 2 lbs. chopped beef tenderloin
- 3 cups beef stock
- 4 sliced garlic cloves
- 1 tsp. black pepper
- 1 tsp. dried oregano
- 1 tsp. dried rosemary
- 1 tsp. sea salt

Directions:
1. Wash the meat with clean water and pat dry with a kitchen paper. Move to a cutting board and chop into bite-sized pieces. Put the meat chops in a large container and put in all the spices. Liberally rub with your hands to allow spice to penetrate into the meat. Save for later.
2. Plug in your instant and coat the stainless steel insert with olive oil. Switch your Instant Pot to "Sauté' mode and put in meat chops and garlic. Cook until golden brown, about 5 minutes.
3. Add the beef broth and securely lock the lid. Close the steam release handle and switch to "Manual' mode. Turn the timer to 20 minutes and cook on "High" pressure.
4. When your instant pot sounds the end signal, release the pressure using the quick release method and open the pot. Move the meat to a serving platter and garnish with some thinly sliced chives and fresh thyme prior to serving.

Nutritional Info:
Calories: 562, Fats: 28.3g, Carbs: 2.4g, Protein: 69.7g

Caribbean Beef

Total time: 60 minutes
Servings: 4

Ingredients:
- 1 cup Water
- 1 tsp. Garlic Powder
- 1 tsp. grated Ginger
- 1 tsp. Thyme
- 2 lbs. Beef Roast (chuck or shoulder)
- 4 whole Cloves
- ¼ tsp. Pepper
- ½ tsp. Salt

Directions:
1. Mix all of the spices and rub into the meat.
2. Stick the cloves into the beef.
3. Put the beef inside the Instant Pot.
4. Pour the water around it.
5. Shut and secure the lid and set it to MANUAL.
6. Switch the Instant Pot to "High" and cook for 45 minutes.
7. Quickly release the pressure
8. Use two forks to shred the beef on a chopping board
9. Serve and enjoy.

Nutritional Info:
Calories: 710, Fats: 1.1g, Carbs: 1.1 g, Protein: 55g

Herbed Sirloin Tip Roast

Total time: 1 hour
Servings: 6

Ingredients:
- 2 tbsps. mixed herbs spice blend (Mrs. Dash)
- Black pepper
- 1 tsp. garlic powder
- 3 lbs. Sirloin tip roast
- 1¼ tsps. paprika
- Salt

Directions:
1. In your instant pot, stir in all ingredients and pour in a cup of water.
2. Put on the lid and seal off the vent.
3. While on Manual option, set timer to 60 minutes.
4. Do natural pressure release.

Nutritional info:
Calories: 394, Fat: 25.4g, Carbs: 1.6g, Protein: 37.7g

Gingered Beef Tenderloin

Total time: 50 minutes
Servings: 8

Ingredients:
- ¼ cup coconut aminos
- 2 tbsps. olive oil
- 4 fillet mignon steaks
- 2 tbsps. thinly sliced ginger or 2 x 1/8 tsp ground ginger
- 2 tbsps. minced garlic or 2 x 3/4 tsp of garlic powder

Directions:
1. Press the Sauté button on the Instant Pot and heat the oil.
2. Sauté the garlic for 1 minute until fragrant.
3. Stir in the ginger and fillet mignon and allow to sear for 4 minutes
4. Season with coconut aminos. Add salt and pepper to taste. Pour a cup of water.
5. Set the lid in place and select the Meat/Stew mode and set timer to 40 minutes.
6. Do natural pressure release.

Nutritional info:
Calories: 199, Fat: 9.8g, Carbs: 1.3g, Protein: 24.8g

Simple Shredded Beef

Total time: 1 hour 20 minutes
Servings: 6

Ingredients:
- 3½ lbs. beef chuck roast
- 2 tbsps. olive oil or carnivore oil of your choosing
- 1 tsp. sea salt
- 2½ cups water

Directions:
1. Preheat the Instant Pot by selecting SAUTÉ. Add the oil.
2. Season the meat with salt.
3. Add the meat and sauté for 8-10 minutes on both sides, until browned.
4. Close and lock the lid. Select the cancel button to reset the cooking program, then select the MANUAL setting and set the cooking time for 75 minutes at HIGH pressure.
5. Once cooking is complete, select CANCEL and let Naturally Release for 10 minutes. Release any remaining steam manually. Uncover the pot.
6. Remove the beef roast from the pot and shred the meat with 2 forks.
7. Return to the Instant Pot and stir with remaining liquid.
8. Serve with cooked rice, potato or pasta. Also you can use the meat in sandwiches, burrito bowls, tacos, and more.

Nutritional Info:
Calories: 160, Fat: 10g, Carbs: 1g, Protein: 16g

Delicious Braised Short Ribs

Total time: 45 minutes
Servings: 8

Ingredients:
- 4 lbs. Beef short ribs.
- ¼ tsp. salt
- 3 garlic cloves
- 1 cup water

Directions:
1. Set the instant pot to the sauté temperature and spread the fat across the bottom. When it is heated, add the beef and sauté for 5 minutes.
2. Now add the garlic, salt, and 1 cup water, close the lid and cook for 35 minutes.
3. When cooking is done, serve on the bone or pull meat from bones.
4. Serve with rice or as you like most

Nutritional info:
Calories: 340, fat: 19g, Carbs: 1.8g, protein: 22g.

Pot Roast

Total time: 1 hour and 20 minutes.
Servings: 8

Ingredients:
- 3 lbs. Beef chuck
- 1 tbsp. cooking oil.
- 1 cup water
- 2 bay leaves
- Lemon pepper or seasoning of your choice

Directions:
1. Season the roast with lemon pepper and set aside.
2. Set the instant pot to sauté and place the oil into it. When the oil is heated, add the meat and brown both sides. Remove the meat from the pot.
3. Now add the water and bay leaves. Place the meat on top of the onion. Set the time for 70 minutes at high pressure.
4. Remove the lid and thicken as you want.

Nutritional info:
Calories: 240, fat: 19g, Carbs: 2g, protein: 25g.

Sage Beef

Total time: 50 minutes
Servings: 4

Ingredients:
- 1 tbsp. chopped sage
- 2 tbsps. olive oil or carnivore oil of your choosing
- Black pepper
- 2 lbs. cubed beef stew meat
- 2 cups beef stock
- 2 minced garlic cloves
- Salt

Directions:
1. Set your instant pot on Sauté mode, add the oil, heat it up, add the garlic and sauté for 5 minutes.
2. Brown the meat for 5 more minutes.
3. Mix in the remaining ingredients, put the lid on and cook on High for 30 minutes.
4. Release the pressure naturally for 10 minutes, divide the mix between plates and serve.

Nutritional Info:
Calories: 263, fat: 14g, carbs: 1.7g, protein 15g

Oregano Spiced Beef Chops

Total time: 30 minutes
Servings: 3

Ingredients:

- 1 tsp. dried dill
- 1 lb. beef chops
- 1 tsp. dried parsley
- ½ tsp. coriander
- 1 tsp. thyme
- 1 tsp. oregano
- 1 tbsp. olive oil or carnivore oil of your choosing
- ¼ cup water
- ½ tsp. salt

Directions:

1. Combine the thyme, oregano, dill, parsley, coriander, salt, and olive oil in a mixing bowl. Stir the mixture and mix the chops with the spice mix.
2. Close the top lid and seal its valve.
3. Press "MANUAL" setting. Adjust cooking time to 25 minutes.
4. Allow the recipe to cook for the set cooking time.
5. After the set cooking time ends, press "CANCEL" and then press "NPR (Natural Pressure Release)".
6. Instant Pot will slowly and naturally release the pressure.
7. Open the top lid, add the cooked recipe mix in serving plates.
8. Serve and enjoy!

Nutritional Info:

Calories: 326, Fat: 17.5g, Carbs: 2.1g, Protein – 46g

Tasty Beef Brisket

Total time: 1 hour 10 minutes
Servings: 6

Ingredients:
- 3 lbs. brisket
- 1 tsp. salt
- 1 tsp. black pepper
- 2 tbsps. carnivore oil of your choosing
- 2 cups beef stock
- 1 bay leaf

Directions:
1. Season beef with salt and pepper. Heat oil in Instant Pot on Sauté mode. Brown brisket on both sides and transfer to a plate.
2. Add celery to the pot. Brown lightly, then add bay leaf. Replace beef in pot.
3. Close lid and set cooking time to 50 minutes.
4. Discard bay leaf and season sauce to taste with salt and pepper.

Nutritional Info:
Calories: 528, Fat: 24.47 g, Carbs: 2 g, Protein: 74.9g

Instant Pot Beef Steak

Total Time: 35 minutes
Servings: 2

Ingredients:
- ½ lb. beef steak (short loin or top loin)
- 1 tbsp. coriander powder
- 1 tbsp. fresh lemon juice
- 1 tbsp. cumin powder
- 1½ tbsps. oil
- 1 tbsp. turmeric powder
- 1 tbsp. red chili powder
- 1 tbsp. vinegar
- Salt

Directions:
1. Combine each with the spices, vinegar and oil and lemon juice in the very large bowl.
2. Add the beef to the prepared mixture, mix well and marinate it overnight.
3. Select the *Meat/Chicken* mode on the Power Pressure Cooker XL and place for thirty minutes.
4. Add a cupful of water towards the heating pot and hang the steamer trivet inside.
5. Arrange the marinated beef on the trivet.
6. Put on the lid and turn pressure to succeed knob towards the closed position.
7. Once done; release pressure completely and take from the lid. Serve.

Nutritional Info:
Calories: 257, Carbs: 6.8g, Protein: 26.6g, Fat: 13.1g

Chicken

Simple Roast Chicken

Total time: 35 minutes
Servings: 4

Ingredients:
- 4 tbsps. softened butter
- 1 crushed garlic
- Salt
- Black pepper
- 1 tbsp. paprika
- 2 crushed rosemary sprigs
- 2 crushed thyme sprigs
- 2 quarts water
- 1 whole chicken

Directions:
1. Combine the butter, salt, garlic, thyme, black pepper, paprika, and rosemary in a mixing bowl.
2. Pour the water into the inner pot.
3. Pat the chicken dry.
4. Season the chicken with butter mixture evenly then place the chicken in the inner pot.
5. Secure the lid. Choose "Manual" mode. Cook for 20 minutes at High pressure. Once cooking is complete, use a natural pressure release; carefully remove the lid.
6. Afterwards, place the chicken under the broiler for 10 minutes until the skin is lightly crisped. Bon appétit!

Nutritional Info:
Calories: 376, Fat: 18.2g, Carbs: 2g, Protein: 49.1g

Garlicky Greek Chicken

Total time: 26 minutes
Servings: 4

Ingredients:
- 1 tsp. dried oregano
- 1 sliced lemon
- 3 tbsps. extra-virgin olive oil or carnivore oil of your choosing
- 1 lb. chicken thighs
- 3 minced garlic cloves

Directions:
1. Put all ingredients in the Instant Pot.
2. Add ½ cup of water and Apply pepper and salt for seasoning.
3. Set lid in place and ensure vent points to "Sealing."
4. Cook on "Poultry" mode for 20 minutes.
5. Do natural pressure release.

Nutritional info:
Calories: 298, Carbs: 2.1g, Protein: 16.5g, Fat: 23.3g

Classic Lemon Chicken

Total time: 42 minutes
Servings: 4

Ingredients:
- 4 chicken thighs
- 2 tbsps. fresh lemon juice
- 1 sliced onion
- 2 tsps. carnivore oil of your choosing
- 1 crushed garlic clove

Directions:
1. In a mixing bowl, thoroughly mix olive oil and lemon juice.
2. Coat the chicken and add to the baking pan; top with the garlic and onion.
3. Take the Instant Pot and place over dry kitchen surface; open its top lid and switch it on.
4. Pour 1 cup water in the cooking pot area. Arrange the trivet or steamer basket inside it; arrange the pan over the trivet/basket.
5. Close its top lid and make sure that its valve it closed to avoid spillage.
6. Press "MANUAL". Adjust the timer to 30 minutes.
7. Pressure will slowly build up; let the added ingredients to cook until the timer indicates zero.
8. Press "CANCEL". Now press "QPR" to quickly release pressure.
9. Open the top lid, transfer the cooked recipe in serving plates.
10. Serve the recipe warm.

Nutritional info:
Calories: 173, Fat: 11g, Carbs: 2g, Protein: 14g

Instant Pot Garlic Chicken

Total time: 42 minutes
Servings: 4

Ingredients:
- Pepper
- 5 minced garlic cloves or seasoning of choice
- Salt.
- 4 halved chicken breasts skin on or cuts of your choice
- 3 tbsps. carnivore oil of your choosing

Directions:
1. Select the Sauté button on the Instant Pot and heat the cooking oil. Sauté the garlic until fragrant then stir in the chicken breasts. Apply pepper and salt for seasoning.
2. Stir for 5 minutes then pour in water.
3. Put on the lid and seal off the vent. While on Manual option, set timer to 30 minutes.
4. Do natural pressure release.

Nutritional info:
Calories: 591, Fat: 37.5g, Carbs: 1.1g, Protein: 60.8g

Whole Roasted Chicken with Lemon and Rosemary

Total time: 13 hours
Servings: 8

Ingredients:
- 1 whole chicken
- 1 sliced lemon
- Pepper and salt
- 1 rosemary sprig
- 6 minced garlic cloves

Directions

1. Place the whole chicken in a big bowl and rub all the spices onto the surface and insides of the chicken. Set in your refrigerator to marinate for about 2 hours.
2. Place the chicken in the Instant Pot and pour a cup of water.
3. Put on the lid and seal off the vent. While on Manual option, set timer to 60 minutes.
4. Do natural pressure release.

Nutritional info:
Calories: 248, Fat: 17.2g, Carbs: 0.9g, Protein: 21.3g

Easy Asian Chicken

Total time: 27 minutes
Servings: 5

Ingredients:
- 3 minced garlic cloves
- ¼ cup organic chicken broth
- 1½ lbs. boneless chicken breasts skin on or cuts of your choice
- 1 tbsp. ginger slices

Directions:
1. Place all ingredients in the Instant Pot. Give a good stir.
2. Set lid in place and ensure vent is sealed.
3. Press the Poultry button and adjust the cooking time to 15 minutes.
4. Do natural pressure release.
5. Once the lid is open, press the Sauté button and allow to simmer until the sauce has reduced. Garnish with chopped scallions and drizzle with sesame oil if desired.

Nutritional info:
Calories: 169, Fat: 3.6g, Carbs: 1.2g, Protein: 30.9g

Smoky Paprika Chicken

Total time: 30 minutes
Servings: 8

Ingredients:
- 2 tbsps. smoked paprika
- 2 lbs. chicken breasts skin on or cut of your choice
- Salt.
- Pepper
- 1 tbsp. olive oil or carnivore oil of your choosing

Directions:
1. Select the Sauté button on the Instant Pot and heat the olive oil. Stir in the chicken breasts and smoked paprika for 3 minutes until lightly golden.
2. Apply pepper and salt for seasoning and pour in ½ cup water.
3. Put on the lid and seal off the vent.
4. While on Manual option, set timer to 25 minutes.
5. Do natural pressure release.
6. Garnish with cilantro or scallions if desired.

Nutritional info:
Calories: 217, Fat: 12.4g, Carbs: 1.5g, Protein: 34g

Slow Cooked Chicken Drumstick

Total time: 8 hours
Servings: 12

Ingredients:
- ¼ tsp. dried thyme
- 1½ tbsps. paprika
- Black pepper
- Salt
- 12 chicken drumsticks

Directions:
1. Place all ingredients in the Instant Pot. Give a good stir to coat the entire chicken with the spices.
2. Close the lid and do not seal the Vent.
3. Press the Slow Cooker button and adjust the cooking time to 8 hours.

Nutritional info:
Calories: 218, Fat: 12.1g, Carbs: 2g, Protein: 23.8g

Slow Cooked Spiced Whole Chicken

Total time: 1 hour
Servings: 12

Ingredients:
- Black pepper
- Salt
- 1 sliced onion or 1 tbsp of onion powder
- 1 whole chicken
- 2 thyme sprigs
- 1 tsp. ground chilies

Directions:
1. In your instant pot, add in all ingredients and massage the chicken to coat with the spices.
2. Pour a cup of water.
3. Put on the lid and seal off the vent.
4. While on Manual option, set timer to 60 minutes.
5. Do natural pressure release.

Nutritional info:
Calories: 249, Fat: 17.9g, Carbs: 1.2g, Protein: 21.7g

Instant Pot Crispy Chicken

Total time: 25 minutes
Servings: 8

Ingredients:
- Pepper
- 1 tbsp. paprika
- 1 tsp. rosemary leaves
- Salt
- 2 lbs. chicken wings

Directions:
1. Place all ingredients in the Instant Pot. Add in water and stir to combine everything.
2. Put on the lid and seal off the vent.
3. While on Manual option, set timer to 10 minutes.
4. Do natural pressure release.
5. Take the chicken out of the Instant Pot and place them in a baking sheet lined with foil.
6. Bake in the oven at 400°F for 10 minutes

Nutritional info:
Calories: 148, Fat: 4.1g, Carbs: 1.1g, Protein: 25.2g

Filipino Chicken

Total time: 25 minutes
Servings: 4

Ingredients:
- 5 lbs. chicken thighs
- Salt
- ½ cup white vinegar
- Black pepper
- 1 tsp. crushed black peppercorns
- 4 minced garlic cloves
- 3 bay leaves
- ½ cup soy sauce

Directions:
1. Set the Instant Pot on Poultry mode, add the chicken, vinegar, soy sauce, salt, pepper, garlic, peppercorns, and bay leaves, stir, cover, and cook for 15 minutes.
2. Release the pressure for 10 minutes, uncover the Instant Pot, discard the bay leaves, stir, divide the chicken between plates, and serve.

Nutritional Info:
Calories: 430, Fat: 19.2g, Carbs: 2g, Protein: 76g

Roasted Chicken

Total time: 45 minutes
Servings: 8

Ingredients:
- 1 whole chicken
- 1 tbsp. extra virgin olive oil
- Salt
- 1½ tbsps. lemon zest
- 1 cup chicken stock
- 1 tbsp. fresh thyme
- ½ tsp. ground cinnamon
- Black pepper
- 1 tbsp. cumin
- 2 tsp. garlic powder
- 1 tbsp. coriander

Directions:
1. In a bowl, mix the cinnamon with cumin, garlic, coriander, salt, pepper, and lemon zest and stir well.
2. Rub chicken with half of the oil, then rub it inside and out with spice mix. Set the Instant Pot on Sauté mode, add the rest of the oil and heat it up.
3. Brown the chicken evenly for 5 minutes
4. Add the stock and thyme, stir, cover and cook on the Poultry setting for 25 minutes. Release the pressure naturally and transfer chicken to a platter.
5. Add the cooking liquid over it, and serve.

Nutritional Info:
Calories: 260, Fat: 3.1g, Carbs: 2.1g, Protein: 26.7

Lemon Herb Whole Chicken

Total time: 30 minutes
Servings: 4

Ingredients:
- 3 tsps. Salt
- 3 tsps. Garlic powder
- 2 tsps. Dried rosemary
- 2 tsps. Dried parsley
- 1 tsp. Pepper
- 1 Whole chicken
- 2 tbsps. carnivore oil of your choosing
- 1 cup water
- 1 zested and quartered lemon

Directions:
1. In a bowl, mix pepper, parsley, rosemary, garlic, and salt.
2. Rub the chicken with the mixture.
3. Press Sauté and add oil to the Instant Pot.
4. Add chicken and brown for 5 to 7 minutes.
5. Press Cancel and remove the chicken.
6. Add broth and deglaze the pot.
7. Place lemon quarters inside the chicken and sprinkle the chicken with lemon zest.
8. Place chicken back into the pot.
9. Close the lid and press Meat.
10. Cook on High for 25 minutes.
11. Do a natural release when done.
12. Slice the chicken and serve.

Nutritional Info:
Calories: 861, Fat: 62.9g, Carb: 2g, Protein: 45.5g

Barbecue Wings

Total time: 17 minutes
Servings: 4

Ingredients:
- 1 lb. Chicken wings
- 1 tsp. Salt
- ½ tsp. Pepper
- ¼ tsp. Garlic powder
- 1 cup Sugar-free barbecue sauce
- 1 cup water

Directions:
1. In a bowl, mix wings, half of the sauce, garlic powder, salt, and pepper.
2. Add water into the Instant Pot and place a steam rack.
3. Place wings on the steam rack and close the lid.
4. Press Manual and cook 12 minutes on High.
5. Do a quick release, remove and toss in remaining sauce.
6. If you want crispier wings, then broil the wings for 5 to 7 minutes in the oven.

Nutritional Info:
Calories: 237, Fat: 14.9g, Carb: 1g, Protein: 19.9g

Shredded Chicken Breast

Total time: 30 minutes
Servings: 4

Ingredients:
- 2 chicken breasts. You can leave the skin on but it won't shred that easy or simply add 1 tbsp of carnivore oil of your choosing to add more fat
- ½ tsp. black pepper
- ½ tsp. salt
- ½ cup water

Directions:
1. Rub the chicken with the black pepper and salt evenly.
2. Add the chicken breasts to the Instant Pot and pour the chicken broth.
3. Close and lock the lid. Select MANUAL and cook at HIGH pressure for 8 minutes.
4. Once cooking is complete, use a Natural Release for 10 minutes, then release any remaining pressure manually.
5. Shred the chicken and serve hot

Nutritional Info:
Calories: 90.1, Fat: 2g, Carbs: 1g, Protein: 17g

Curried Chicken

Total time: 25 minutes
Servings: 4

Ingredients:
- 1½ lbs. Chicken drumsticks
- 1 tsp. Salt
- 1 tbsp. curry powder.
- ½ tsp. Dried thyme
- 1 cup water

Directions:
1. Rub the drumsticks with salt and curry powder.
2. Place rest of the ingredients and chicken into the Instant Pot.
3. Press Manual and cook 20 minutes on High.
4. Do a natural release and serve.

Nutritional Info:
Calories: 284, Fat: 14.11g, Carb: 1.4g, Protein: 31.3g

Italian Chicken Thighs

Total time: 25 minutes
Servings: 4

Ingredients:
- 4 chicken thighs
- 2 minced garlic cloves
- 1 tsp. Salt
- ¼ tsp. Pepper
- ¼ tsp. Dried basil
- ¼ tsp. Dried parsley
- ½ tsp. Dried oregano
- 1 cup water

Directions:
1. Place chicken in a bowl.
2. Rub the chicken with all the spices, herbs, and seasoning.
3. Add water to the Instant Pot and place steam rack.
4. Place chicken thighs on the steam rack and close the lid.
5. Press Manual and cook 15 minutes on High.
6. Do a quick release and remove.
7. Broil chicken in the oven for 3 to 5 minutes if you want crispy chicken.

Mojo Chicken

Total time: 45 minutes
Servings: 4

Ingredients:
- 1 tbsp. fresh lemon Juice
- 1 tbsp. Olive oil or carnivore oil of your choosing
- Black pepper
- 1 cup chicken stock
- 1 Whole chicken
- 2 tbsps. chopped Rosemary
- Salt
- 1 Bay Leaf

Directions:
1. Select the sauté function then add cooking oil.
2. Add the chicken and sauté evenly then put aside
3. Put in the trivet then add all the ingredients.
4. Select the poultry button and cook for 25 minutes
5. Remove the bay leave then serve hot

Nutritional Info:
Calories: 250, Protein: 30g, Fat: 31g, Carbs: 1 g

Italian Shredded Chicken

Total time: 15 minutes
Servings: 8

Ingredients:
- 1 tbsp. Italian Seasoning Mix
- 4 lbs. Chicken Skin on Breasts
- ½ tsp. Salt
- ½ tsp. Black Pepper
- 1 cup water

Directions:
1. Season the chicken evenly then put in the instant pot
2. Add water and cook for 10 minutes under high pressure
3. Shred the chicken then serve warm

Nutritional Info:
Calories: 170, Fat: 7 g, Carbs: 1 g, Protein: 27 Grams

Tasty Simple Chicken Thighs

Total time: 35 minutes
Servings: 8

Ingredients:
- 5 lbs. chicken thighs
- 4 minced garlic cloves
- ½ cup soy sauce
- 1 tsp. black peppercorns
- 3 bay leaves
- ½ tsp. salt
- ½ tsp. ground black pepper

Directions:
1. Add the garlic, vinegar, peppercorns, bay leaves, salt and pepper to the Instant Pot and stir well.
2. Add the chicken thighs. Stir to coat the chicken.
3. Close and lock the lid. Click the poultry function and set the cooking time for 15 minutes.
4. Once timer goes off, allow to Naturally Release for 10 minutes. Unlock the lid.
5. Remove the bay leaves, stir and serve.

Nutritional Info:
Calories: 188, Fat: 6.2g, Carbs: 1.8g, Protein: 29.5g

Pork

Mustard Pork Chops

Total time: 32 minutes
Servings: 2

Ingredients
- 2 Pork chops
- ½ tsp. Paprika
- ½ tsp. Thyme
- 1 tsp. Apple cider vinegar
- 1 tbsp. Mustard
- 1 tbsp. Olive oil
- ½ cup chicken stock
- 2 tbsps. Lemon juice
- Black pepper
- Salt

Directions:
1. Rub pork chops with paprika, thyme, pepper, and salt.
2. Press Sauté and add oil to the Instant Pot.
3. Add pork chops and cook for 2 to 3 minutes on both sides, or until slightly brown.
4. In a bowl, mix stock, vinegar, mustard, and lemon juice. Add to the Instant Pot.
5. Cook on High for 15 minutes with the lid closed
6. Open and do a natural release.
7. Serve.

Nutritional Info:
Calories: 331, Fat: 27.2g, Carb: 2g, Protein: 19.1g

Leyna's Blend Pork Chops

Total time: 35 minutes
Servings: 2

Ingredients

- 1 tbsp. cooking oil.
- 2 boneless Pork chops
- ½ tbsp. Butter.
- ½ tsp. Crushed red pepper.
- ¼ tsp. Dried parsley.
- ¼ tsp. Garlic powder.
- ¼ tsp. Chili powder.
- ¼ tsp. Dried basil.
- ¼ tsp. Salt.
- ¼ tsp. black pepper.
- 2 tbsps. Hot sauce.
- ½ cup water

Directions:

1. Press Sauté and melt the oil in the Instant Pot.
2. Add pork chops and brown on both sides.
3. Add water, butter, black pepper, salt, basil, chili powder, garlic powder, parsley, and red pepper.
4. Close the lid and cook 30 minutes on High.
5. Do a natural release.
6. Open the pork chops and rub with hot sauce.
7. Serve.

Nutritional Info:

Calories: 232, Fat: 19.9g, Carb: 0.8g, Protein: 12.2g

Basil-Lime Carnitas

Total time: 30 minutes
Servings: 2

Ingredients:
- 1 tbsp. Avocado oil or carnivore oil of your choosing
- ½ lb. chopped Pork shoulder
- ¼ tsp. Dried oregano.
- ¼ tsp. Chili powder.
- ¼ tsp. Ground cumin.
- ¼ tsp. Dried basil.
- ¼ tsp. Salt.
- ¼ tsp. Black pepper.
- ¼ tsp. Lime juice.
- ½ cup. Water

Directions:
1. Press Sauté and heat the oil.
2. Add the pork and brown it.
3. Add salt, black pepper, basil, cumin, chili powder, oregano, and water.
4. Close the lid and hit Cancel.
5. Press Manual and cook 25 minutes on High.
6. Do a natural release.
7. Open and stir in lime juice.
8. Shred the meat and serve.

Nutritional Info:
Calories: 344, Fat: 25.3g, Carb: 1.1g, Protein: 26.7g

Asian Lemongrass Pork

Total time: 1 hour
Servings: 10

Ingredients:
- 2 lbs. pork shoulder
- ¼ cup fish sauce
- 4 tbsps. coconut oil or carnivore oil of your choosing
- 2 tbsps. lemongrass
- 6 garlic cloves

Directions:
1. Press the "Sauté" button on the Instant pot and heat the coconut oil.
2. Sauté the garlic and lemongrass until fragrant.
3. Cook the pork chunks for 3 mins, stirring, until all sides are seared.
4. Season with fish sauce and pour in a cup of water.
5. Set lid in place and ensure vent points to "Sealing."
6. Press the "Meat/Stew" button and adjust the time to 55 minutes.
7. Do natural pressure release.

Nutritional info:
Calories: 249, Carbs: 0.8g, Protein: 21.5g, Fat: 23.3g

Smothered Pork Chop

Total time: 30 minutes
Servings: 3

Ingredients:
- 1 tbsp. ghee or carnivore oil of your choosing
- 3 pork chops
- 1 cup water
- Black pepper
- 1 tsp. garlic powder
- ½ tsp. onion powder
- 1 tbsp. paprika
- Salt

Directions:
1. Press the "Sauté" button and melt the ghee. Once hot, sear the pork chops until golden browned, about 4 minutes per side.
2. Add the water, garlic powder, onion powder, paprika, salt, and black pepper to the inner pot.
3. Secure the lid. Choose the "Manual" mode and cook for 10 minutes at High pressure. Once cooking is complete, use a natural pressure release; carefully remove the lid.
4. Serve the pork chops warm

Nutritional Info:
Calories: 472, Fat: 28.8g, Carbs: 1.1g, Protein: 42.7g

Adobo Pork Chops

Total time: 55 minutes
Servings: 5

Ingredients:
- 3 tbsps. carnivore oil of your choosing
- 1 lb. pork chops
- ¼ cup freshly squeezed lemon juice
- 3 minced garlic cloves
- ½ cup coconut aminos

Directions:
1. Place all ingredients in the Instant Pot.
2. Apply a seasoning of pepper and salt and add ¼ cup of water.
3. Set lid in place and ensure vent points to "Sealing."
4. Press the "Meat/Stew" button and adjust the time to 50 minutes.
5. Do natural pressure release.

Nutritional info:
Calories: 271, Carbs: 2 g, Protein: 18.2g, Fat: 23.3g

Smokey and Spicy Instant Pot Roast

Total time: 1 hour 30 minutes
Servings: 12

Ingredients:
- 1 tbsp. cayenne pepper flakes
- 5 tbsps. carnivore oil of your choosing
- Salt
- 2 tbsps. liquid smoke
- Pepper
- 4 lbs. pork butt

Directions:
1. Place all ingredients in the Instant Pot.
2. Pour in a cup of water.
3. Set lid in place and ensure vent points to "Sealing."
4. Press the "Meat/Stew" button and adjust the time to 1 hour and 30 minutes.
5. Do natural pressure release.

Nutritional info:
Calories: 456, Carbs: 0.7g, Protein: 32.9g, Fat: 39g

Delicious Pork Chops

Total time: 20 minutes
Servings: 4

Ingredients:
- 4 boneless pork chops
- 1 tbsp. or carnivore oil of your choosing
- Black pepper
- 3 tbsps. melted ghee or butter
- 1 cup chicken stock
- Salt
- ¼ tsp. sweet paprika

Directions:
1. Set your instant pot on sauté mode, add the oil, heat it up, add pork chops and brown for a few minutes on each side.
2. Add ghee, salt, pepper, paprika and stock, stir, cover pot and cook on High for 5 minutes.
3. Serve your pork chops and enjoy

Nutritional Info:
Calories: 362, fat: 4g, carbs 1g, protein 19

Kalua Pork

Total time: 1 hour 40 minutes
Servings: 5

Ingredients:
- 4 lbs. pork shoulder
- ½ cup water
- 2 tbsps. carnivore oil of your choosing
- Black pepper
- 1 tbsp. liquid smoke
- Salt

Directions:
1. Set the Instant Pot on Sauté mode, add the oil, and heat it up.
2. Add the pork, salt, and pepper, brown for 3 minutes on each side, and transfer to a plate.
3. Stir the liquid smoke and water into the Instant Pot.
4. Return the meat, stir, cover the Instant Pot and cook on the Meat/Stew setting for 90 minutes.
5. Release the pressure for 15 minutes, transfer the meat to a cutting board and shred it with 2 forks.
6. Divide the pork on plates, add some of the sauce on top, and serve hot

Nutritional Info:
Calories: 243, Fat: 15g, Carbs: 1g, Protein: 26g

Pork Carnitas

Total time: 1 hour 30 minutes
Servings: 12

Ingredients:
- 1 ½ tbsps. Salt
- 1 tbsp. Oregano
- 2 tsp. Ground Cumin
- 1 tsp. Black Pepper
- 6 lbs. Pork Butt Roast
- ½ tsp. Chili Powder
- ½ tsp. Ground Paprika
- 2 tbsps. carnivore oil of your choosing
- ¼ cup Water
- 4 minced garlic cloves

Directions:
1. Season your pork butt with all seasoning, and then allow it to marinate for three hours. Press sauté, and then add in your oil. Roast your pork for five minutes per side.
2. Add all of your remaining ingredients in, and then cook on high pressure for ninety minutes.
3. Use a quick release, and shred your meat before serving warm with sauce. You can serve on bread or over rice. \

Nutritional Info:
Calories: 314, Fat: 14g, Carbs: 2g, Protein: 41g

Mexican Pulled Pork

Total time: 1 hour 30 minutes
Servings: 15

Ingredients:
- 1 tsp. cinnamon
- 4 lbs. pork shoulder
- 2 tsps. garlic powder
- 5 tbsps. carnivore oil of your choosing
- 1 tsp. cumin powder

Directions:
1. In your instant pot, add all ingredients. Top with 1 ½ cups of water.
2. Apply pepper and salt for seasoning.
3. Set lid in place and ensure vent points to "Sealing."
4. Press the "Meat/Stew" button and adjust the time to 1 hour and 30 minutes.
5. Do natural pressure release.
6. Once the lid is open, take the meat out and shred using two forks.

Nutritional info:
Calories: 364, Carbs: 0.5g, Protein: 20.4g, Fat: 35.9g

Italian Pork Cutlets

Total time: 1 hour
Servings: 6

Ingredients:
- 4 tbsps. olive oil
- Salt
- 6 pork cutlets
- Black pepper
- 1 tbsp. Italian herb mix

Directions:
1. In your instant pot, add in all ingredients. Top with 1½ cups of water.
2. Set lid in place and ensure vent points to "Sealing."
3. Press the "Meat/Stew" button and adjust the time to 55 minutes.
4. Do natural pressure release.

Nutritional info:
Calories: 322, Carbs: 0.9g, Protein: 19.4g, Fat: 34.6g

Mexican Chili Pork

Total time: 55 minutes
Servings: 6

Ingredients:
- 2 tsps. ground cumin
- 1 tbsp. red chili flakes
- 3 tbsps. olive oil or carnivore oil of your choosing
- 2 lbs. sliced pork sirloin
- 2 tsps. minced garlic

Directions:
1. Press the "Sauté" button on the Instant pot and heat the olive oil.
2. Sauté the garlic until fragrant.
3. Add the pork sirloin and stir for 3 minutes.
4. Add the cumin and chili flakes.
5. Pour in a cup of water and Apply pepper and salt for seasoning.
6. Set lid in place and ensure vent points to "Sealing."
7. Press the "Meat/Stew" button and adjust the time to 50 minutes.
8. Do natural pressure release.

Nutritional info:
Calories: 159, Carbs: 0.8g, Protein: 21.1g, Fat: 16.8g

Indian Instant Pot Slow Roasted Pork

Total time: 8 hours
Servings: 6

Ingredients:
- 1 tsp. cumin
- 1 lb. pork loin
- ½ cup carnivore oil of your choosing
- 2 chopped garlic cloves

Directions:
1. Place the pork loin in the Instant Pot and set aside.
2. In a food processor, place the remaining ingredients and Apply pepper and salt for seasoning.
3. Pulse until smooth then pour over the pork loin.
4. Set lid in place and ensure vent points to "Venting."
5. Press the "Slow Cook" button and adjust the time to 8 hours.

Nutritional info:
Calories: 321, Carbs: 0.6g, Protein: 19.5g, Fat: 26.5g

Slow Cook Garlic Pork Tenderloin

Total time: 8 hours
Servings: 10

Ingredients:
- 3 lbs. pork tenderloin
- 1 tsp. thyme
- 3 tbsps. extra-virgin olive oil or carnivore oil of your choosing
- 1 minced garlic cloves
- ¼ cup butter

Directions:
1. Heat the oil and butter in the Instant Pot.
2. Sauté the garlic and thyme until fragrant.
3. Add the pork tenderloin and cook for 3 mins, stirring.
4. Pour in a cup of water and Apply pepper and salt for seasoning.
5. Set lid in place and ensure vent points to "Venting."
6. Press the "Slow Cook" button and adjust the time to 8 hours.

Nutritional info:
Calories: 252, Carbs: 0.2g, Protein: 11.8g, Fat: 35.6g

BBQ Baby Back Ribs

Total time: 1 hour
Servings: 6

Ingredients:
- 2 lbs. baby back ribs
- 1 tsp. salt
- ½ tsp. black pepper
- ½ tsp. garlic powder
- 1 cup water
- Barbecue sauce

Directions:
1. Remove the membrane from the back of the ribs.
2. In a large bowl, combine salt, pepper, garlic powder, and onion powder.
3. Add the ribs and rub all sides with the spice mix.
4. Prepare the Instant Pot by adding the water and bourbon to the pot and placing the steam rack in it.
5. Place the ribs on the steam rack and secure the lid.
6. Press the manual button and set the cooking time for 20 minutes at HIGH pressure.
7. When the timer beeps, use a Natural Release for 10 minutes, then release any remaining pressure manually. Open the lid.
8. Preheat the oven to broil.
9. Arrange the ribs onto a baking tray and brush on all sides with the BBQ sauce.
10. Place under the broiler for 5-10 minutes. Serve.

Nutritional Info:
Calories: 257, Fat: 13.9g, Carbs: 2g, Protein: 24.9g

Braised Pork Belly

Total time: 1 hour 10 minutes
Servings: 2

Ingredients:
- 1 lb. pork belly
- 1 tbsp. carnivore oil of your choosing
- Black pepper
- 1 minced garlic clove
- Salt
- Rosemary sprig

Directions:
1. Press the sauté setting on the Instant Pot and heat the oil.
2. Add the pork belly and sauté for 2 minutes per side, until starting to brown.
3. Season the meat with salt and pepper, add the garlic.
4. Add the rosemary sprig.
5. Bring to a boil and press the CANCEL key to stop the SAUTÉ function.
6. Choose the MANUAL setting and set the cooking time for 35 minutes at HIGH pressure.
7. Once cooking is complete, use a Natural Release for 10 minutes, then release any remaining pressure manually. Open the lid.
8. Slice the meat and serve.

Nutritional Info:
Calories: 295, Fat: 20g, Carbs: 2g, Protein: 17g

Smoked Pork Shoulder

Total time: 1 hour 30 minutes
Servings: 6

Ingredients:
- 3 lbs. pork shoulder
- 2 tbsps. carnivore oil of your choosing
- 3 chopped garlic cloves
- Black pepper
- 1 cup water
- Salt
- 2 tbsps. liquid smoke

Directions:
1. Press the SAUTÉ setting on the Instant Pot and heat the oil.
2. Add the garlic and sauté for 1 minute.
3. Season the meat with salt and pepper to taste.
4. Add the pork shoulder to the pot and cook for 5 minutes on both sides, until browned.
5. Pour in the water and liquid smoke and deglaze the pot by scraping the bottom to remove all of the brown bits. Close and lock the lid.
6. Select the CANCEL button to reset the cooking program, then select the MANUAL setting and set the cooking time for 70 minutes at HIGH pressure.
7. Once cooking is complete, let the pressure Release Naturally for 10 minutes. Release any remaining steam manually. Uncover the pot.
8. Transfer the pork to a plate and shred the meat.
9. Serve warm

Nutritional Info:
Calories: 201, Fat: 14g, Carbs: 2g, Protein: 17g

Turkey

Saucy Turkey Drumsticks

Total time: 30 minutes
Servings: 5

Ingredients

- 2 lbs. turkey drumsticks
- 12 oz. Ultra Light beer or chicken stock
- Salt
- 1 medium-sized leek, sliced
- 2 garlic cloves, sliced
- Black pepper
- ½ tsp. ground allspice
- 2 sprigs rosemary, chopped
- 2 bay leaves

Directions:

1. Add all ingredients to the inner pot.
2. Secure the lid. Choose the "Manual" mode and cook for 20 minutes at High pressure. Once cooking is complete, use a natural pressure release; carefully remove the lid.
3. You can thicken the pan juices if desired. Enjoy!

Nutritional Info:

Calories: 394, Fat: 17.3g, Carbs: 3.7g, Protein: 50.1g

Herbed Mayonnaise Roast Turkey

Total time: 35 minutes

Servings: 8

Ingredients:
- 3 lbs. turkey breasts
- 4 smashed garlic cloves
- 2 thyme sprigs
- 2 rosemary sprigs
- 1 cup mayonnaise (recommended from a quality source)
- 2 tsps. salt
- 1 tsp. crushed peppercorns
- 2 tbsps. softened ghee or butter
- 1 sliced lemon

Directions:
1. Pat the turkey dry. In a mixing dish, thoroughly combine the garlic, thyme, rosemary, mayonnaise, salt, peppercorns, and ghee.
2. Rub the mayonnaise mixture all over the turkey breasts.
3. Add a steamer rack and 1/2 cup of water to the bottom of your Instant Pot. Throw in the lemon slices.
4. Secure the lid. Choose the "Manual" mode and cook for 20 minutes at High pressure. Once cooking is complete, use a natural pressure release; carefully remove the lid.
5. Let your turkey stand for 5 to 10 minutes before slicing and serving.

Nutritional Info:
Calories: 393, Fat: 25g, Carbs: 1.9 g, Protein: 39.2g

Aromatic Turkey

Total time: 50 minutes
Servings: 8

Ingredients:
- 1½ cups Chicken Broth
- 1 Bay Leaf
- 1 tsp. Basil
- 1 tsp. Garlic Powder
- 1 tsp. Onion Powder
- 2 lbs. cubed Turkey Breasts
- 2 Thyme Sprigs
- 2 tsp. Sage

Directions:
1. Spray the pot with cooking spray then cook the turkey on sauté mode to a brown color.
2. Put in all other ingredients then close the lid and select manual mode
3. Cook on high pressure for 25 minutes
4. Use natural pressure once cooked
5. Serve the turkey warm with your favorite accompaniment.

Nutritional Info:
Calories: 250, Fats: 18g, Carbs: 2.1g, Protein: 31g

Easy Turkey Roast

Total time: 60 minutes
Servings: 5

Ingredients:
- 2 lbs. turkey breast
- 3 tbsps. Dijon mustard
- 3 tbsps. garlic infused oil (carnivore oil of your choosing with 3 tbsps garlic powder)
- 4 cups chicken stock
- ¼ cup olive oil or omit completely
- 1 tsp. white pepper, but black pepper is ok.
- 2 tsps. sea salt

Directions:
1. Put the meat in the pot and put in chicken stock. Shut and secure the lid and set the steam release handle.
2. Switch your Instant Pot to "Manual" mode and cook for 25 minutes. When finished, depressurize using the quick release method and open the lid. Take the meat out of the pot and save for later.
3. Prepare the baking sheet with a parchment paper as you preheat the oven to 425°F
4. In a small container, whisk together garlic infused oil, olive oil, Dijon, salt, and pepper. Slightly coat the meat with this mixture and place on a baking sheet.
5. Roast for 15 minutes on each side.
6. Remove from the oven and serve instantly.

Nutritional Info:
Calories: 458, Fats: 25.4g, Carbs: 0.9g, Protein: 54.1g

Garlicky and Lemony Turkey

Total time: 25 minutes
Servings: 4

Ingredients:
- ¼ tsp. Paprika
- ½ cup water
- 1¼ lbs. cubed Turkey Breasts
- 1 diced onion
- 1 tbsp. Ghee
- 1 tsp. Salt
- 5 minced garlic cloves
- 1 lemon, juice and zest.

Directions:
1. Melt the ghee in your Instant Pot using the "Sauté" mode.
2. Cook the onions until soft.
3. Put in the water, lemon juice and zest, paprika, and salt.
4. Stir to mix and put in the turkey cubes.
5. Close and lock the lid.
6. Switch your instant pot to "Poultry" mode and allow to cook on DEFAULT.
7. Release the pressure using the quick release method.
8. Serve warm

Nutritional Info:
Calories: 539, Fats: 24g, Carbs: 1.8g, Protein: 50g

Smoked Slow-Cooked Turkey

Total time: 4hours
Servings: 4

Ingredients:
- 1½ lbs. Turkey Breast
- 1 cup Chicken Stock
- 1 tbsp. Dijon Mustard
- 1 tsp. Liquid Smoke
- Black pepper
- 1 tsp. minced Garlic
- 2 tbsps. Sugar Free BBQ Sauce
- 2 tsps. Smoked Paprika
- 4 tbsps. Olive Oil
- Salt

Directions:
1. Switch the Instant Pot to "Sauté" mode and heat the oil.
2. Put in turkey and cook it on all sides, until brown.
3. Mix half of the stock with the rest of the ingredients and pour this mixture over the turkey.
4. Shut and secure the lid and switch your Instant Pot to "Slow Cook" mode.
5. Cook for 2 hours.
6. Release the pressure using the quick release method and pour the rest of the broth over.
7. Shut and secure the lid and slow cook for additional 2 hours.
8. Depressurize quickly.
9. Let sit for a few minutes prior to serving.

Nutritional Info:
Calories: 400, Fats: 30g, Carbs: 2g, Protein: 39g

Spiced Turkey

Total time: 1 hour
Servings: 4

Ingredients:
- 2 crushed garlic cloves
- 2 lbs. turkey breast
- 3 cups chicken stock
- ¼ cup carnivore oil of your choosing
- 1 tsp. dried basil
- 3 whole cloves
- ½ tsp. stevia powder

Directions:
1. Wash the turkey breast under running water and pat dry with a kitchen towel. Transfer into a large Ziploc bag and put in basil, cloves, and oil. Pour in one cup of chicken broth and seal the bag. Shake thoroughly and refrigerate for 20 minutes.
2. Oil-coat the stainless steel insert with some oil and put in garlic. Stir-fry for 2 minutes. Take the turkey out of the fridge and place in the pot along with 2 tbsps. of the marinade and the rest of the chicken broth.
3. Shut and secure the lid and set the steam release handle. Push the 'Manual' button and turn the timer to 25 minutes.
4. When finished, depressurize using the natural release method.

Nutritional Info:
Calories: 313, Fats: 20.3g, Carbs: 2g, Protein: 20.3g

Sweet Turkey Drumsticks

Total time: 40 minutes
Servings: 5

Ingredients:
- ½ cup Soy Sauce
- ½ cup Water
- ½ tsp. Garlic Powder
- 1 tsp. Pepper
- 1 tsp. Salt
- 2 tsps. Sugar Free Sweet and sour
- 6 turkey Drumsticks

Directions:
1. Mix the spices in a small container.
2. Massage the mixture onto the turkey.
3. Mix the water and soy sauce in the Instant Pot.
4. Put in the drumsticks and shut and secure the lid.
5. Switch the Instant Pot to "Manual" mode and cook for 25 minutes.
6. Depressurize for 10 minutes.
7. Your dish is ready! Have fun!

Nutritional Info:
Calories 209, Fats: 15g, Carbs: 2g, Protein: 34g

Buttered Turkey Breast

Total time: 40 minutes
Servings: 6

Ingredients:
- 1 sliced celery stalk
- 1 sliced onion
- 2 cups chicken stock
- 3 crushed garlic cloves
- 3 lbs. turkey breast
- 4 tbsps. butter
- 1 tsp. Salt
- 1 thyme sprig
- ¼ smoked paprika
- ½ tsp. garlic powder

Directions:
1. In a small container, mix salt, garlic powder, onion powder, and smoked paprika. Save for later.
2. Thoroughly wash the meat and place on a clean work surface. Using a sharp knife, cut each piece lengthwise to create a pocket. Stuff each with celery, garlic, and onions. Liberally run with spices and move to the pot.
3. Pour in the stock and put in thyme sprig. Shut and secure the lid and set the steam release handle to the "Sealing" position.
4. Switch your Instant Pot to "Manual" mode and turn the timer to 20 minutes on high pressure.
5. When finished, depressurize using the natural release method and open the lid. Stir in the butter and let it sit, covered, for some time prior to serving.

Nutritional Info:
Calories: 320, Fats: 11.7g, Carbs: 2.1g, Protein: 39.3g

Turkey Leg with Garlic

Total time: 55 minutes
Serving: 1

Ingredients:
- 1 turkey leg
- 2 tbsps. olive oil or carnivore oil of your choice
- 3 cups chicken stock
- 4 crushed garlic cloves
- 1 tbsp. garlic paste
- 1 tsp. salt
- 2 tsps. dried thyme
- 2 tsps. dried oregano
- ¾ tsp. white pepper

Directions:
1. Mix together crushed garlic, garlic paste, oregano, thyme, salt, and pepper. Combine thoroughly and liberally rub over turkey leg. Tightly cover in a large piece of plastic foil and refrigerate for 30 minutes (up to an hour).
2. Remove from the fridge and place in the pot. Pour in the stock and shut and secure the lid. Make sure the steam release handle is on the "Sealing" position and switch to "Manual' mode.
3. Turn the timer to 15 minutes on high pressure.
4. When finished, depressurize using the quick release method and open the lid. Remove the leg along with the stock from the pot and save for later.
5. After that coat the inner pot with olive oil and Switch your Instant Pot to "'Sauté" mode. Put the leg back to the pot to brown for about 2 minutes on each side.
6. Take out of the pot and serve.

Nutritional Info:
Calories 629, Fats: 39.7g, Carbs: 2g, Protein: 62.2g

Turkey Breast with Gorgonzola Sauce

Total time: 45 minutes
Servings: 5

Ingredients:

- 1 ½ cup chicken broth
- 1 lb. chopped turkey skin on breast
- 2 cups heavy cream
- 2 tbsps. butter
- 2 tbsps. oil
- ¼ cup sliced parsley
- ½ cup chopped gorgonzola
- 1 tsp. dried thyme
- 1 tsp. garlic powder
- ¼ tsp. dried oregano
- ½ tsp. onion powder

Directions:

1. Wash thoroughly the meat and pat dry with a kitchen towel. Put on a large cutting board and chop into bite-sized pieces. Move to a large container. Coat thoroughly with spices and save for later.
2. Turn on your Instant Pot and Switch your Instant Pot to "'Sauté" mode. Oil-coat the inner pot with oil and put in the meat. Briefly cook for 4-5 minutes, stirring continuously and pour in the broth. Push the "Cancel" button and shut and secure the lid.
3. Make sure the steam release handle is on the "Sealing" position and switch to "Manual' mode. Cook for 13 minutes on high pressure.
4. When finished, depressurize using the natural release method for 10-15 minutes and then move the pressure valve to the "Venting" position to release any rest of the pressure.
5. Open the lid and remove any rest of the broth. Switch your Instant Pot to "Sauté' mode and put in butter.
6. Stir in heavy cream and gorgonzola. Sauté for about 2 minutes or until the cheese melts.
7. Drizzle with parsley and serve instantly.

Nutritional Info:

Calories: 480, Fats: 37.6g, Carbs: 2.3g, Protein: 32.9g

Instant Turkey Breast

Total time: 45 minutes
Servings: 7

Ingredients:
- 6½ lbs. Turkey breast
- Salt
- 2 cups Chicken stock.
- Pepper
- 1 celery stalk
- 1 thyme sprig

Directions:
1. Mix the turkey with salt and pepper very well.
2. Place the trivet in the instant pot and add the celery, thyme, onion and chicken stock. Now add the turkey and set the time to 30 minutes at high pressure.
3. The turkey should cook completely, if not then cook for 3 to 5 minutes more.
4. Add chicken stock then cook until done.
5. Slice the turkey and serve.

Nutrition info:
Calories: 119, fat: 1g, Carbs: 0g, protein: 28g.

Turmeric Turkey Breast

Total time: 35 minutes
Servings: 4

Ingredients:
- 2 tbsps. carnivore oil of your choice
- Black pepper
- 1 lb. cubed skin on turkey breast
- Salt
- 1 tsp. turmeric powder
- 1 cup chicken stock

Directions:
1. Choose Sauté mode and add the oil to heat.
2. Brown the meat evenly for 5 minutes
3. Mix in all other ingredients and set select high pressure mode for 20 minutes
4. Serve warm once cooked

Nutritional Info:
Calories: 283, fat: 11g, carbs: 2, protein: 15

Basil Turkey Breast

Total time: 30 minutes
Servings: 4

Ingredients:
- 1 lb. cubed turkey breasts
- 1 tbsp. chopped basil
- 4 minced garlic cloves
- ¼ cup chicken stock

Directions:
1. Put everything in the instant pot and put on the lid
2. Set the instant pot on high pressure for 20 minutes
3. Once cooked, release the pressure and serve warm

Nutritional Info:
Calories: 220, fat: 8g, carbs: 2g, protein 15g

Classic Honey Turkey

Total time: 25 minutes
Servings: 6

Ingredients:
- ½ cup water
- 1 tsp. black pepper
- 2 tsps. honey
- ½ tsp. garlic powder
- 6 turkey drumsticks
- ½ cup chicken stock
- 1 tbsp. kosher salt

Directions:
1. Season the meat with the garlic powder, pepper, salt, and honey.
2. Switch on your instant pot after placing it on a clean and dry kitchen platform.
3. Pour the water into the cooking pot area. Arrange the trivet inside it; arrange the meat over the trivet.
4. Close the pot by closing the top lid. Also, ensure to seal the valve.
5. Press "Manual" cooking function and set cooking time to 20 minutes. It will start cooking after a few minutes. Let the pot mix cook under pressure until the timer reads zero.
6. Turn off and press "Cancel" cooking function. Allow the inside pressure to release naturally; it will take 8-10 minutes to release all inside pressure.
7. Open the pot and serve on a serving plate or bowl. Enjoy the Paleo dish!

Nutritional Info:
Calories: 126, Fat: 4g, Carbs: 2g, Protein: 19g

Rosemary Turkey

Total time: 30 minutes
Servings: 4

Ingredients:
- 3 tbsps. soy sauce
- 1 tbsp. Dijon-style mustard
- 1 lb. turkey tenderloin
- 2 tsps. dried rosemary
- 1/3 cup water

Directions:
1. Combine the rosemary, soy sauce, and mustard in a bowl.
2. Put everything in the instant pot
3. Put on the lid and press poultry function and cook for 18 minutes.
4. Select cancel and click on NRP for 10 minutes
5. Remove the lid and serve warm.

Nutritional Info:
Calories: 134, Fat: 29g, Carbs: 2.5g, Protein: 19g

Instant Pot Turkey Breast Tenderloin

Total time: 15 minutes
Servings: 2

Ingredients:
- 2 turkey breast tenderloin
- ¼ tsp. thyme
- 1 tsp. garlic powder
- 1 tsp. salt
- ½ tsp. rosemary
- 1 cup water
- ¼ tsp. sage
- ¼ tsp. pepper

Directions:
1. Season the turkey breast with the spices then put in the instant pot
2. Close lid and select poultry function then cook for 7 minutes
3. Release the pressure quickly then remove the lid.
4. Slice the turkey breast and serve warm.

Nutritional Info:
Calories: 376, Fat: 5g, Carbs: 2g, Protein: 79g

Instant Pot Rotisserie Turkey Legs

Total time: 30 minutes
Servings: 4

Ingredients:
- 4 turkey legs
- ½ tsp. pepper
- 1 tbsp. oregano
- 1 tbsp. paprika
- 2 tbsps. carnivore oil of your choice
- 1 tsp. salt
- 1 cup water
- 1 tbsp. garlic powder

Directions:
1. Put all the seasonings in a bowl then rub the turkey leg with oil evenly.
2. Coat the turkey legs with the seasoning mixture
3. Pour water at the bottom of the instant pot
4. Put the spiced turkey legs in the instant pot then cook on high for 25 minutes
5. Select NPR for 10 minutes then quickly release the remaining pressure

Nutritional Info:
Calories: 215, Fat: 15.5g, Carbs: 2g, Protein: 16.2g

Tasty Turkey Bites

Total time: 36 minutes
Servings: 4

Ingredients:
- 1 lb. skin on turkey breast
- 3 tbsps. carnivore oil of your choice
- Salt
- 1 cup chicken stock
- 5 minced garlic cloves
- 8 chopped basil leaves
- Black pepper

Directions:
1. Rub the turkey with salt and pepper evenly.
2. Select the *Meat/Chicken* mode and set 25 minutes.
3. Add oil and turkey in the pot. Cook until brown from each part.
4. Stir in garlic and basil. Sauté for 1 minute then add the chicken stock
5. Secure the lid and turn pressure knob for the closed position.
6. Once done; release pressure completely and take off the lid. Give a mild stir and serve warm.

Nutritional Info:
Calories: 358, Carbs: 1.5g, Protein: 36.5g, Fat: 18.3g

Yummy Turkey Thighs

Total time: 50 minutes
Servings: 4

Ingredients:
- 4 turkey thighs
- ½ cup chicken stock
- 2 tbsps. carnivore oil of your choice
- Salt
- 8 minced garlic cloves
- 2 tsps. chopped thyme
- 2 tsps. chopped oregano
- Black pepper

Directions:
1. Rub the turkey thighs with salt and pepper.
2. Select the *Meat/Chicken* mode and set 45 minutes
3. Add the oil and turkey for the heating pot. Cook until brown.
4. Stir in all remaining ingredients.
5. Secure the lid and turn the load knob on the closed position.
6. Once done; release pressure to have success completely and get rid of the lid.

Nutritional Info:
Calories: 544g, Carbs: 2g, Protein: 66.7g, Fat: 24.1g

Fish

Poached Salmon

Total time: 8 minutes
Servings: 2

Ingredients:
- ½ chopped Garlic clove
- 2 salmon fillets (wile caught)
- ¼ tsp.salt
- 4 tbsps. Softened butter
- 1 sliced lemon
- 1 tsp. Dijon mustard.
- ¼ tsp. black pepper
- ½ tsp. ground thyme.
- ¼ tsp.dried parsley

Directions:
1. Add 1-inch water into the Instant Pot.
2. Place the trivet.
3. Place the salmon in an aluminum foil and top with lemon slices.
4. Fold to make a pocket and place on the trivet.
5. Close and cook on Steam for 3 minutes.
6. Meanwhile, melt the butter in the microwave then add salt, pepper, parsley, thyme, garlic, and mustard. Mix well.
7. Do a quick release when done, open, and discard the lemon slices.
8. Serve salmon with sauce.

Nutritional Info:
Calories: 472, Fat: 35.3g, Carbs: 2g, Protein: 35.2g

Sockeye Salmon

Total time: 9 minutes
Servings: 2

Ingredients:
- ½ tsp. Garlic powder
- ¾ cup water
- ½ minced garlic clove
- ½ tsp. Dijon mustard
- Pepper
- 4 oz. salmon fillets
- ½ tbsp. lemon juice
- Salt

Directions:
1. Combine the lemon juice, minced garlic, garlic powder, onion powder, and mustard in a small bowl.
2. Brush the mixture over the salmon.
3. Add water into the pot and lower the rack.
4. Arrange the salmon on the rack and close the lid.
5. Cook on High for 4 minutes.
6. Do a quick pressure release
7. Serve.

Nutritional Info:
Calories: 195, Fat: 10g, Carbs: 1g, Protein: 24g

Dijon Halibut

Total time: 8 minutes
Servings: 2

Ingredients:
- ¾ cup water
- 2 Halibut fillets
- ¾ tbsp. Dijon mustard

Directions:
1. Pour the water into the IP.
2. Brush the halibut with Dijon and place it in the steaming basket.
3. Lower the basket and close the lid.
4. Cook on High for 3 minutes.
5. Do a quick pressure release.
6. Serve.

Nutritional Info:
Calories: 190, Fat: 2g, Carbs: 0.1g, Protein: 40g

Smoked Codfish with Scallions

Total time: 10 minutes
Servings: 3

Ingredients:
- 3 tbsps. chopped scallions
- 3 tsps. butter
- ½ cup water
- Ground black pepper
- 1 sliced lemon
- 3 fillets smoked codfish
- Sea salt

Directions:
1. Place the lemon and water in the bottom of the Instant Pot. Place the steamer rack on top.
2. Place the cod fish fillets on the steamer rack. Add the butter, scallions, salt, and black pepper.
3. Secure the lid. Choose the "Steam" mode and cook for 3 minutes at Low pressure. Once cooking is complete, use a quick pressure release; carefully remove the lid.
4. Serve warm and enjoy!

Nutritional Info:
Calories: 203, Fat: 4.8g, Carbs: 1.5g, Protein: 36.3g

Salmon Meatballs Soup

Total time: 16 minutes
Servings: 5

Ingredients:
- 2 minced garlic cloves
- 2 cups hot water
- 1 lb. ground salmon
- 2 beaten large eggs
- 2 tbsps. butter

Directions:
1. In a bowl, mix butter, garlic, eggs and salmon. Apply a seasoning of pepper and salt.
2. Combine the mixture and use your hands to form small balls.
3. Place the fish balls in the freezer to set for 2 hours or until frozen.
4. Pour the hot water in the Instant Pot and drop in the frozen fish balls.
5. Apply pepper and salt for seasoning.
6. Set lid in place and ensure vent is on "Sealing."
7. On "Manual" mode, set timer to 10 minutes.

Nutritional info:
Calories: 199, Carbs: 0.6g, Protein: 13.3g, Fat: 19.4g

Steamed Lemon Salmon

Total time: 9 minutes
Servings: 2

Ingredients:
- Salt
- 2 frozen salmon fillets
- Cooking spray
- Pepper
- ¼ cup lemon juice

Directions:
1. Pour 1 cup water into the Instant Pot.
2. Add steam rack inside.
3. Spray rack with oil.
4. Add salmon fillets on top.
5. Season with salt and pepper.
6. Drizzle with lemon juice.
7. Cove;r the pot and choose steam function.
8. Cook for 3 minutes.

Nutritional info:
Calories: 172, Fat: 6.7g, Carbs: 2g, Protein: 24.6g

Salmon with Basil Pesto

Total time: 6 hours 6 minutes

Servings: 6

Ingredients:
- 2 tbsps. fresh lemon juice
- 1½ lbs. salmon fillets
- ½ cup olive oil or carnivore oil of your choice
- 2 cups basil leaves
- 3 minced garlic cloves

Directions:
1. Set basil leaves, oil, lemon juice, and garlic in a food processor.
2. Apply pepper and salt for seasoning.
3. Adjust the moisture by adding a few tablespoons of water and pulse until smooth.
4. Place the salmon fillets in the Instant Pot and add the pesto sauce.
5. Set lid in place and ensure vent points to "Venting."
6. Press the "Slow Cook" button and adjust the time to 6 hours.

Nutritional info:
Calories: 336, Carbs: 0.9g, Protein: 20.5 g, Fat: 28.1g

Super Simple Quick Shrimp

Total time: 2 minutes

Servings: 4

Ingredients:
- 32 Oz Bag frozen large peel on raw shrimp
- 1 Cup Water
- 2 lemons or 2 tbsp Lemon juice
- 1/4 cup All purpose Seasoning of your choice

Directions:
1. Add frozen shrimp to Instant Pot.
2. Pour in water, lemon juice, or juice lemons (toss them in as well).
3. Add seasoning and mix and break apart any shrimp that together. If some are still stuck that's ok.
4. Set to "manuel" high pressure for 2 minutes.
5. When finished you can quick release.

Nutritional info:
Calories: 281, Carbs: 1.6g, Protein: 25.4g, Fat: 27.9g

Steamed Chilli-Rubbed Tilapia

Total time: 16 minutes
Servings: 4

Ingredients:
- 2 tbsps. chili powder
- 1 lb. skinless tilapia fillet
- Salt
- ½ tsp. garlic powder
- 2 tbsps. carnivore oil of your choice
- Pepper

Directions:
1. Set a trivet in your Instant Pot and pour a cup of water into the pot.
2. Season the tilapia fillets with salt, pepper, chili powder, and garlic powder. Drizzle with oil on top.
3. Place on the steamer basket and close the lid. Make sure that the vent is sealed.
4. Select the Steam option and set timer to 10 minutes.
5. Do quick pressure release.

Nutritional info:
Calories: 211, Fat: 10g, Carbs: 2g, Protein: 26g

Lemon Dill Salmon

Total time: 10 minutes
Servings: 2

Ingredients:
- 2 Salmon filets
- 1 tsp. Chopped dill
- ½ tsp. Salt
- ¼ tsp. Pepper
- 1 cup water
- 2 tbsps. Lemon juice.
- ½ sliced lemon

Directions:
1. Season the salmon with salt, pepper, and dill.
2. Add water to the Instant Pot and place steam rack.
3. Place salmon on the steam rack (skin side down).
4. Drizzle with lemon juice and put lemon slices on top.
5. Close the lid and press Steam.
6. Cook 5 minutes on High.
7. Do a quick release and serve with lemon slices and dill.

Nutritional Info:
Calories: 127, Fat: 4.9g, Carb: 1.5g, Protein: 17.1g

Foil Pack Salmon

Total time: 10 minutes
Servings: 2

Ingredients:
- 2 Salmon fillets
- 1 tsp. Salt
- ¼ tsp. Pepper
- ¼ tsp. Garlic powder
- ¼ tsp. Dried dill
- ½ sliced lemon
- 1 cup water

Directions:
1. Place salmon on a square of foil, skin side down.
2. Season with seasoning and drizzle with lemon juice.
3. Place lemon slice on each filet.
4. Pour water in the Instant Pot and place a steam rack.
5. Place foil packets on the steam rack and close the lid.
6. Press Steam and cook 7 minutes.
7. Do a quick release.
8. Serve.

Nutritional Info:
Calories: 125, Fat: 4.6g, Carb: 0.4g, Protein: 18.5g

Lamb

Lamb Stew with Bacon

Total time: 38 minutes
Servings: 2

Ingredients:
- ¼ tsp. dried rosemary
- 2 garlic cloves
- Salt
- 2 chopped bacon slices
- 1 cup beef broth
- ½ lb. chopped lamb leg
- ½ tbsp. butter.
- Black pepper

Directions:
1. Press Sauté and melt the butter in the Instant Pot.
2. Add bacon and cook for 3 minutes. Press Cancel.
3. Meanwhile, rub the meat with garlic and spices.
4. Place in the Instant Pot and add broth.
5. Cover and cook on High for 25 minutes.
6. Do a natural release.
7. Open and serve.

Nutritional Info:
Calories: 453, Fat: 23.6g, Carbs: 1.8g, Protein: 52.6g

Rosemary Lamb

Total time: 1 hour
Servings: 8

Ingredients:
- 2 lamb shanks
- 2 chopped onions
- 2 bay leaves
- 3 cups beef stock
- 2 rosemary sprigs

Directions:
1. Take the Instant Pot and place over dry kitchen surface; open its top lid and switch it on.
2. Press "SAUTÉ". Grease the pot with some cooking oil.
3. Add the meat; stir-cook for 4-5 minutes to evenly brown. Set aside.
4. Stir in onions and allow to cook for 4 minutes until turn translucent and softened.
5. Add the lamb and then the broth.
6. Add the remaining ingredients and stir well.
7. Put on the lid and ensure the valve is closed.
8. Press "MANUAL". Adjust the timer to 40 minutes.
9. Pressure will slowly build up; let the added ingredients to cook until the timer indicates zero.
10. Press "CANCEL". Now press "QPR" to quickly release pressure.
11. Open the top lid, transfer the cooked recipe in serving plates.
12. Remove the rosemary sprigs and bay leaves. Serve the recipe warm.

Nutritional info:
Calories: 318, Fat: 17g, Carbs: 3g, Protein: 37g

Chili Lamb Leg

Total time: 1 hour
Servings: 4

Ingredients:
- 3 tbsps. carnivore oil of your choice
- 2 choppedred chili peppers
- 2 lbs. boneless and choppedlamb leg
- 2 cups beef stock
- 3 crushed garlic cloves
- 2 tsps. chili powder
- ½ tsp. groundblack pepper
- 1 thyme sprig
- 1 tsp. salt

Directions:
1. Thoroughly wash the meat thoroughly under cold running water and pat dry with a kitchen towel.
2. Rub thoroughly with oil and garlic. Drizzle with salt, pepper, and chili powder. Tightly cover with aluminum foil and refrigerate for 30 minutes.
3. After that plug in the instant pot and remove the meat from the fridge. Put in the pot and put in beef stock. Put in thyme sprig and chopped chili peppers.
4. Shut and secure the lid and set the steam release handle to the "Sealing" position. Switch your Instant Pot to "Manual" on high pressure for 20 minutes.
5. Naturally the pressure with natural release method and open the lid.
6. Serve instantly.

Nutritional Info:
Calories 524, Fats: 27.4g, Carbs: 0.9g, Protein: 65.2g

Crispy Garlic Lamb Chops

Total time: 30 minutes
Servings: 4

Ingredients:
- ¼ cup soy sauce
- 2 cups water
- 4 lamb chops
- 3 crushed garlic cloves
- 4 tbsps. butter
- ½ tsp. smoked paprika
- 1 tsp. salt
- ½ tsp. garlic powder
- ½ tsp. ground mustard
- 1 tsp. ground black pepper

Directions:
1. Put the meat in the pot and pour in the stock. Shut and secure the lid and set the steam release handle to the "Sealing" position. Switch your Instant Pot to "Manual" mode and cook for 15 minutes on high pressure.
2. When finished, depressurize using the quick release method and open the lid. Remove the chops from the pot and save for later.
3. Remove the liquid and Switch your Instant Pot to "'Sauté" mode. Heat up the inner pot and then put in butter. Put in chops and brown for 3-4 minutes on one side. Turnover and continue to cook for an additional 2-3 minutes. Remove from the pot.
4. Put in garlic and pour in the soy sauce. Sprinkle with spices and cook for an additional 4-5 minutes, stirring continuously.
5. Push the "Cancel" button and put in browned chops. Coat thoroughly with the sauce and serve.

Nutritional Info:
Calories 331, Fats: 20g, Carbs: 2.4g, Protein: 33.9g

Lamb Riblets

Total time: 45 minutes
Servings: 4

Ingredients:
- 3 crushed garlic cloves
- 5 cups water
- 1 tbsp. lemon juice
- 2 lbs. lamb riblets
- 4 tbsps. ghee
- ¼ cup chopped coriander
- 2 wholecloves
- 1 tsp. salt
- 2 tsps. chili powder

Directions:
1. Wash thoroughly the meat and place in the pot. season with salt and chili pepper and pour in the broth.
2. Put in lemon juice and cloves. Shut and secure the lid and set the steam release handle to the "Sealing" position.
3. Switch your Instant Pot to "Manual" mode and cook for 40 minutes on high pressure. If you want, you can also slow cook for 6-8 hours.
4. Release the pressure with natural release method and open the lid. Remove the cloves and mix in ghee. Drizzle with coriander and serve instantly

Nutritional Info:
Calories 375, Fats: 22.8g, Carbs: 1.9g, Protein: 38.1g

Heavy Balsamic Lamb Shoulder

Total time: 45 minutes
Servings: 5

Ingredients:
- 2 tbsps. butter
- 1 cup water
- 2 tbsps. soy sauce
- 1 tbsp. Dijon mustard
- ¼ cup balsamic vinegar
- 2 lbs. lamb shoulder
- 3 crushed garlic cloves
- ¼ cup swerve
- 1 tsp. salt
- ½ tsp. black pepper
- 1 tsp. dried sage

Directions:
1. Turn on your Instant Pot and Switch your Instant Pot to "'Sauté" mode. Oil-coat the inner pot with butter and heat up.
2. Put in garlic and briefly cook – for 1 minute. After that pour in the soy sauce and balsamic vinegar, Dijon, and swerve. Stir vigorously and cook for 2-3 minutes.
3. Push the "Cancel" button and save for later.
4. Wash the lamb with clean water and rub with salt, pepper, and sage. Move to the pot and pour in the stock.
5. Shut and secure the lid and set the steam release handle to the "Sealing" position.
6. Switch your Instant Pot to "Manual" mode on high pressure for 35 minutes
7. Naturally release the pressure with the natural release method and open the lid. Move the meat to a large platter and drizzle with the sauce from the pot.
8. Serve instantly.

Nutritional Info:
Calories 425, Fats: 19.4g, Carbs: 1.3g, Protein: 56.9g

Ginger Lamb

Total time: 40 minutes
Servings: 4

Ingredients:
- 2 lbs. cubed lamb shoulder
- 1 tbsp. grated ginger
- 2 tbsps carnivore oil of your choice
- Black pepper
- 1 tsp. ground cumin
- Salt
- 1 tsp. paprika
- 1 cup beef stock

Directions:
1. Select Sauté mode, add the oil, to heat.
2. Add the ginger, cumin, and the paprika and sauté for 5 minutes.
3. Brown the meat for 5 minutes
4. Toss in the remaining ingredients and cook for 20 minutes on High manual setting.
5. Natural Release for 10 minutes and serve warm.

Nutritional Info:
Calories: 211, fat: 9g, carbs: 1.8g, protein 12g

Spicy Pulled Lamb

Total Time: 1 hour 35 minutes
Servings: 4

Ingredients:
- 2 lbs. boneless lamb shoulder
- 2 tbsps. olive oil or carnivore oil of your choice
- 2 cups chicken stock
- 1 tsp. minced garlic
- 1 sprig rosemary
- 1 tsp. dried oregano
- 3 minced green chilies
- Salt
- 2 tbsps. chopped parsley

Directions:
1. Set to Sauté, heat oil and sear lamb on both sides until brown, 5 minutes. Transfer to a plate and set aside.
2. Pour stock into inner pot, scrape the bottom to deglaze, and mix in the garlic.
3. Return lamb to pot and top with rosemary, oregano, green chilies, and salt. Seal the lid, select Pressure Cook on High, and set time to 60 minutes.
4. Do a natural release for 15 minutes.
5. Unlock the lid, shred lamb with two forks, adjust the taste with and stir in parsley.

Nutritional Info:
Calories: 447, Fat: 27g, carbs: 2g, Protein: 47g

Braised Lamb Shanks (Contains more than normal carbs)

Total Time: 1 hour 15 minutes
Servings: 4

Ingredients:
- 2 tbsps. carnivore oil of your choice
- 2 lbs. lamb shanks
- Black pepper
- 6 minced garlic cloves
- ¾ cup red wine
- Salt
- 1 cup chicken broth
- 2 cups crushed tomatoes
- 1 tsp. dried oregano

Directions:
1. Set to Sauté, heat oil, season with lamb with salt and pepper, and sear until brown, 3 minutes per side.
2. Transfer to a plate. Stir in garlic and sauté about 30 seconds.
3. Mix in red wine and cook for 2 minutes while stirring and scraping the bottom of any attached bits. Add tomatoes and oregano. Stir and cook for 2 minutes.
4. Return lamb to pot and baste with sauce. Seal the lid, select Manual/Pressure Cook on High, and set time to 45 minutes.
5. After cooking, allow a natural release for 15 minutes, then a quick pressure release to let out the remaining steam.
6. Unlock the lid, stir in parsley, and adjust taste with salt and pepper. Divide between plates and serve.

Nutritional info:
Calories: 523, Fat: 21g, Carbs: 2.1g, Protein: 58g

Classic Lamb Tagine

Total Time: 60 minutes
Servings: 4

Ingredients:
- 2 tbsps. ghee or butter
- Salt
- 1½ lbs. cubed lamb stew meat
- 6 minced garlic cloves
- 1 lemon, zested and juiced
- 2 bay leaves
- Black pepper
- 2 tsps. cumin powder
- 2 tsps. coriander powder
- 2 tsps. ginger powder
- ½ tsp. turmeric
- ¼ tsp. cinnamon powder
- ¼ tsp. clove powder
- ¼ tsp. red chili flakes
- 2 cups water

Directions:
1. Set to Sauté, melt ghee and cook lamb until brown on the outside, 6 to 7 minutes. Add garlic and cook 5 minutes.
2. Stir in lemon zest, bay leaves, salt, black pepper, cumin, coriander, ginger, turmeric, cinnamon, clove powder, and red chili flakes. Cook until fragrant, 1 to 2 minutes. Mix in water.
3. Seal the lid, select Pressure Cook on High, and set time to 20 minutes. After cooking, allow a natural release for 10 minutes.
4. Unlock the lid, and adjust the taste. Discard bay leaves and stir in green olives and parsley.
5. Serve into bowls.

Nutritional Info:
Calories: 286, Fat: 11g, Carbs: 1.8g, Protein: 32g

CPSIA information can be obtained
at www.ICGtesting.com
Printed in the USA
LVHW050747141120
671607LV00009B/383